The Glowworm Who Lost Her Glow

Crabtree Publishing Company
www.crabtreebooks.com

PMB 16A, 350 Fifth Avenue,
Suite 3308,
New York, NY 10118

616 Welland Avenue,
St. Catharines, Ontario
Canada, L2M 5V6

For Rebecca Price
W.B.

Cataloging-in-Publication data is available at the Library of Congress.

Published by Crabtree Publishing in 2006
First published in 2004 by Egmont Books Ltd.
Text copyright © William Bedford 2004
Illustrations copyright © Sophie Joyce 2004
The Author and Illustrator have asserted their moral rights.
Paperback ISBN 0-7787-2652-5
Reinforced Hardcover Binding ISBN 0-7787-2630-4

The Glowworm Who Lost Her Glow

By William Bedford

Illustrated by Sophie Joyce

Go Bananas

It was a warm summer night and all the girl glowworms in the field were busy glowing. The boy glowworms were busy chasing them. The moon and the stars were glowing on everybody.

But Georgina wasn't glowing.

Georgina the glowworm had

lost her glow.

Without my glow the other

glowworms can't see me in the

dark, she thought sadly. How

will I ever make new friends?

She sat on her branch, and watched
the dawn chase the night across the
sky. The light was pink and opal. The
clouds were like big sheep roaming
through a blue field.

7

A teardrop slid slowly down
Georgina's cheek. In the pale dawn
sunlight, the tear shone like a star.

Ooh!
How pretty!

"Even my teardrops have a glow,"

said Georgina sadly.

The moon yawned sleepily and

went to bed.

"Good morning," said a blackbird, landing in the hedge, the light from the sun brightening his beak. "Why do you look so sad?"

"I've lost my glow," said Georgina. "Have you seen it?"

Oooh-er!

"What's a glow? Is it something to eat?" the blackbird asked.

Does he eat glowworms?

"No!" cried Georgina.

"You don't have to shout," said the blackbird. "How am I supposed to know? I don't glow. I fly." And off he flew.

11

Georgina decided to search for her glow.

Where are you, glow?

She set out across the field.

Dewdrops hung down from the grass,

sparkling in the light from the sun,

like tiny rainbows.

She came to a pond. The sun reflected in the water, like a huge orange beach ball.

"Good morning," croaked a frog, sitting on a leaf and admiring himself in the surface of the pond. "You look unhappy."

"I've lost my glow," said Georgina. "I'm going to look for it."

I'm so gorgeous.

Ugh!

14

"I've never had a glow," said the frog.
"Not that I need one. I'm handsome
enough without a glow. Just look at my
reflection in the water. Don't you think
I'm good-looking?"

"Very," said Georgina, in case he ate her.

"Yes," said the frog. "I look at myself all
day and I never get bored."

Georgina sighed and went on searching. She saw a rooster strutting on top of a farmhouse, its beautiful tail gleaming in the sunlight like a waterfall of feathers.

She saw a pheasant

scurrying across the grass, like

a ball of fire shining in the sun.

She saw sunlight reflecting from the windows of the homes in the village, and the windshields of the cars on the road.

She saw sunlight winking on
a weathervane and dazzling
from the top of a bus.

Cock-a-
doodle-doo!

Wow!

19

Georgina felt very sad. Everything

in the world seemed to be shining,

but Georgina still couldn't glow. So

she crawled into a hole in a bank, to

see if she was glowing in the dark. She

wasn't. She sighed and closed her eyes.

A mole was busy digging a tunnel.

"You look miserable," the mole said.

"I've lost my glow," Georgina told

him. "I don't like the dark. Nobody

can see me when it's dark."

"I don't like light," the mole replied.
"I think you can manage perfectly
well without it."

"But I need to glow," said Georgina.

"Do you mind doing it somewhere
else then," said the mole.

I need
a snooze.

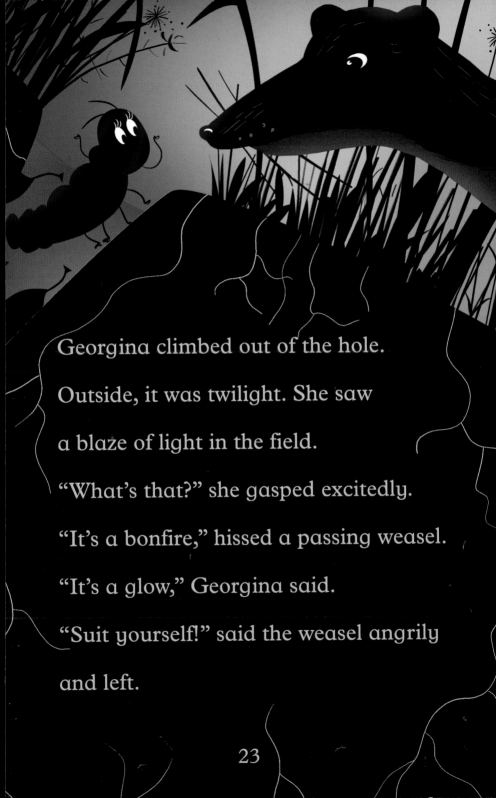

Georgina climbed out of the hole.

Outside, it was twilight. She saw

a blaze of light in the field.

"What's that?" she gasped excitedly.

"It's a bonfire," hissed a passing weasel.

"It's a glow," Georgina said.

"Suit yourself!" said the weasel angrily

and left.

The flames of the bonfire were
dancing in the water of the pond.
It was the most beautiful sight
Georgina had ever seen.

Crowds had gathered around to watch.

Some of them held flashlights, shining

up into the darkness.

Suddenly the sky filled with light.

Shooting stars raced into the darkness.

Fountains of color danced and sparkled.

Pinwheels whizzed and sizzled.

Rockets set off for the moon.

"What is it?" Georgina gasped.

"Fireworks," snuffled a hedgehog.

"They're glowing," Georgina sighed.

"They're noisy," the hedgehog grumbled.

"But what are they for?" asked Georgina.

"It's a midsummer party, down at

the farm," said the hedgehog.

"To celebrate June 21st, the shortest

night of the year."

And then he curled

up and rolled away.

Goodbye

Georgina went down

to the farm.

In the farmyard, she saw the farmer, going to milk the cows. He was carrying a lantern which glowed and shone on the straw in the barn. It was a warm, soft glow, and the cows went "Moo" as if they enjoyed the light.

She climbed up a wall and looked
through the window into the farmhouse.
In the kitchen a big table was laid ready
for the party. A fire was burning in the
hearth, with flames jumping up the
chimney and throwing shadows
around the room.

How
cozy!

On the table was a huge cake, with lots of colored candles around the edge. The candles were not lit. "What are those?" Georgina asked a dormouse who came and sat beside her on the window ledge. "Candles," squeaked the dormouse.

"Do candles glow?" Georgina asked.

"Yes, but not until they're lit," said the dormouse. "They won't light them until the party begins."

"I've never been to a party," Georgina sighed.

"Noisy things," said the dormouse. "But lots of crumbs."

Georgina went back to her hedge feeling very sad. She climbed on to her branch and watched all the girl glowworms glowing around her and all the boy glowworms chasing them. Nobody noticed Georgina. She sat and stared at the moon. It was glowing. She stared at the stars.

Everything is glowing, except me.

could see lights in the village glowing.

The bonfire was a big red glow in the field.

"I am the unhappiest glowworm in the field," Georgina said aloud.

There was a long silence.

somebody appeared.

It was a boy glowworm.

He flew down out of the darkness and landed beside Georgina with a crash.

"Whoops!" he said. "Sorry about that. My name's Samuel. Who are you?"

"I'm Georgina," she replied.

He was very handsome.

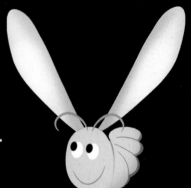

Georgina blushed.

"Do you want to come

to a party?" Samuel

asked her.

"Oh, yes please!" Georgina cried.

She had found a friend at last.

So Georgina and Samuel went

to the party in the farmyard.

I'm flying!

The blackbird and the frog sang lots
of songs, and the rooster clapped
his claws.

The weasel danced with the hedgehog
while the dormouse danced with
the mole.

Inside the farm, the candles were lit

on the cake, and the room glowed

with candlelight.

A choir of crickets and nightingales

sang in the trees, and in the bushes,

all the glowworms glowed.

Georgina and Samuel
danced together beneath the
light of the midsummer night moon.
"Oh, I wish I had a glow like all
the other girls," Georgina said sadly.
"I've been trying to glow all day."

Aaah!

"But look!" cried Samuel. "You are!"

Georgina looked around, and to her

surprise she saw the most wonderful

sight. A beautiful green glow.

"Is that me?" she gasped.

"Of course it's you," Samuel laughed.

And it was!

What is a source of light?

A **source of light** is something that makes its own light – like the **sun**, **light bulbs**, **bonfires**, **fireworks**, **candles**, **stars** . . . and **glowworms**, of course!

When she's fully grown, a female glowworm can make her own light and glow for hours at a time.

I'm a real, live source of light!

Male glowworms can't glow very well.

But we CAN fly!

The sun

The sun is the biggest and most important source of light.

The sun is the source of light for the earth. It makes daylight.

Remember, never look directly at the sun – it will hurt your eyes.

Because the sun is so bright, it's hard to see other sources of light when it's daytime.

The earth

I can't see Georgina's glow very well in the daytime.

What is darkness?

Darkness happens when there is no light. Because we need light to see things with, when it's dark, we can't see anything.

Night happens when our part of the earth moves away from the sun.

Good night.

Most sources of light show up best at nighttime. Can you find six sources of light in this picture?

I look good at night, don't I?

I can't *see* anything in my underground home, because there are no sources of light. But I like the dark! I move around, dig, and find my food by using my *senses* of smell, hearing, and touch.

Try this game with your friends!

Tell your friends to close their eyes, and place a small object in their hands. See if they can tell what it is by touching, hearing, or even smelling it.

Here are some ideas: egg, key, ball, hairclip, eraser, different kinds of fruit and vegetables.

A pin cushion?

Yes!

What is a reflection?

When light hits a shiny surface it bounces back, or is **reflected**. Shiny things like **mirrors, metal, glass,** and **tinfoil** all reflect light.

Here are some shiny things that reflect light. Can you find them in the story?

The moon looks so bright because it reflects the light of the sun.

Did you know that birds called magpies like to collect shiny objects that reflect light? They use them to make their nests look nice and attract partners!

Make your own glittery disco ball!

What you'll need:

1 small round potato

1 piece of string about 12 inches (30cm long)

3 large pieces of tinfoil

glue

1 flashlight

1 adult to help!

Now here's the fun part. Look around the house for all the glittery things you can find! Anything that reflects light really well, like silvery candy wrappers, bottle tops, tinsel, and sequins.

1 First take your potato and ask an adult to tie the string around it like a gift.

2 To make your disco ball, first take one piece of tinfoil and wrap it around your potato like this.

3 Then take the next piece of tinfoil and wrap it over the top of the first piece. Scrunch the foil gently and make a round ball shape.

4 Wrap the final piece of tinfoil around your ball. Scrunch it gently. All the folds and crinkles in the foil will reflect the light and make your disco ball sparkle like the sun!

Get scrunching!

Keep the string poking out like this.

5 Now, use glue to stick your glittery objects to your disco ball.

6 Ask an adult to help you hang it up where everyone can see it.

Now it's party time! Wait until it gets dark (or just shut your curtains), put on your favorite music, and shine a flashlight on your amazing glitter ball!

If you spin it around, it'll look even groovier!

Groovy move!

Rainbows

Have you ever seen a rainbow? Next time it's sunny and rainy at the same time, take a look outside. Rainbows are made when raindrops reflect the sun's light. In fairy tales, if you find the end of the rainbow, you'll discover a pot of shiny gold!

We've found the end of the rainbow!

You can make your very own rainbow!

Ask an adult to place a glass of water on a window sill, on a bright, sunny day.

Ask them to place the glass so that the edge just hangs over the edge of the sill (be careful it doesn't fall off!). A rainbow should form on the floor!

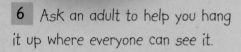